A Fruitcake CHRISTMAS

Also Available

Board Books:
A Fruitcake Christmas
Buzby the Misbehaving Bee
Flo the Lyin' Fly
Flood of Lies
Hermie and the Big Bully Croaker
Hermie: A Common Caterpillar
Rock, Roll, and Run
Stuck in a Stinky Den
The Caterpillars of Ha-Ha
The Twelve Bugs of Christmas
Webster the Scaredy Spider

Picture Books:
Buzby the Misbehaving Bee
Hermie: A Common Caterpillar
Flo the Lyin' Fly
The Twelve Bugs of Christmas (includes DVD)
Webster the Scaredy Spider

Videos & DVDs:
A Fruitcake Christmas
Buzby the Misbehaving Bee
Hermie: A Common Caterpillar
Flo the Lyin' Fly
Webster the Scaredy Spider

Some titles available in Spanish

MAX LUCADO'S
HeRMIe
& Friends™

A Fruitcake
CHRISTMAS

Story by Troy Schmidt

Illustrations by GlueWorks Animation

Based on the characters from the series
Max Lucado's Hermie & Friends™

Tommy
NELSON®
www.tommynelson.com
A Division of Thomas Nelson, Inc.
www.ThomasNelson.com

Text and art copyright © 2005 by Max Lucado.
Story by Troy Schmidt, based on the characters from the series Max Lucado's Hermie & Friends™.

Illustrations by GlueWorks Animation.

Karen Hill, Administrative Editor for Max Lucado.

All rights reserved. No portion of this book may be reproduced in any form without the written permission of the publisher, with the exception of brief excerpts in reviews.

Published in Nashville, Tennessee, by Tommy Nelson®, a Division of Thomas Nelson, Inc. Visit us on the Web at www.tommynelson.com.

Tommy Nelson® books may be purchased in bulk for educational, business, fund-raising, or sales promotional use. For information, please email SpecialMarkets@ThomasNelson.com.

Scripture quotations in this book are from the *International Children's Bible*®, *New Century Version*®, © 1986, 1988, 1999 by Tommy Nelson®, a Division of Thomas Nelson, Inc. All rights reserved.

Library of Congress Cataloging-in-Publication Data

Schmidt, Troy.
    A fruitcake Christmas / story by Troy Schmidt ; illustrations by GlueWorks Animation.
        p. cm.
    Based on the characters from the series Max Lucado's Hermie & Friends™.
    Summary: After Hailey and Bailey show Iggy and Ziggy Cockroach the true meaning of Christmas, all of the garden insects share some of Grannypillar's famous fruitcake.
    ISBN 1-4003-0545-4 (hardcover picture book)
    ISBN 1-4003-0546-2 (hardcover board book)
    [1. Christian life—Fiction. 2. Christmas—Fiction. 3. Insects—Fiction. 4. Fruitcake—Fiction.]
I. GlueWorks Animation. II. Title.
    PZ7.S3565Fru 2005
[E]—dc22   2005010584

Printed in the United States of America
05 06 07 08 09 PHX 5 4 3 2 1

www.hermieandfriends.com
Email us at: comments@hermieandfriends.com

"This is how God showed his love to us:
He sent his only Son into the world to give us life
through him. . . . And God gave us this command:
Whoever loves God must also love his brother."

—1 John 4:9, 21

Christmastime was the happiest time in the garden . . . and the busiest. There were trees to decorate, cards to send, gifts to wrap, and Grannypillar's fruitcake to make—all before the big Christmas Eve celebration.

Everyone was helping. Well, almost everyone . . .

The richest bugs in the garden, Iggy and Ziggy Cockroach, never took time for Christmas. They even made Freddie Flea work harder than ever.

"Christmas just slows you down," Ziggy growled.

"Bah, humbugger," Iggy snarled.

Behind the cockroaches trudged poor Freddie, carrying a heavy load of fruit and nuts.

The Ladybug twins, Hailey and Bailey, asked Hermie, "How'd Iggy and Ziggy get so rich?"

"All year long they grab up food and take it to their mansion," Hermie said.

"They're so greedy, there's not much left for anyone else," Wormie added.

Then Hermie and Wormie remembered:
It was almost time to watch the ants move
Grannypillar's scrumptious fruitcake to the
center of the garden.

"Let's go!" said Hermie. And off they went
to Grannypillar's.

The twins went to tell their mother about Iggy and Ziggy.

"Maybe they don't understand what Christmas is all about," Lucy Ladybug said.

"You mean making wish lists and getting gifts?" Hailey asked.

"And eating fruitcake?" Bailey added.

"No," Lucy said. "Christmas is not about fruitcake or getting and giving. It's about Jesus."

"At Christmas we celebrate God's gift to us," Lucy said. "God sent His Son, Jesus, to the earth, and whoever loves Him will get to live in heaven forever."

"Wow! God must really love us," Hailey said.

Lucy hugged her girls. "He does."

Meanwhile, Hermie and Wormie had reached Grannypillar's. She usually had lots of delicious food to eat, but not this year. Those greedy cockroaches, Iggy and Ziggy, had taken almost all the fruit and nuts for themselves. But somehow Grannypillar had managed to make her famous fruitcake as big and tasty as ever.

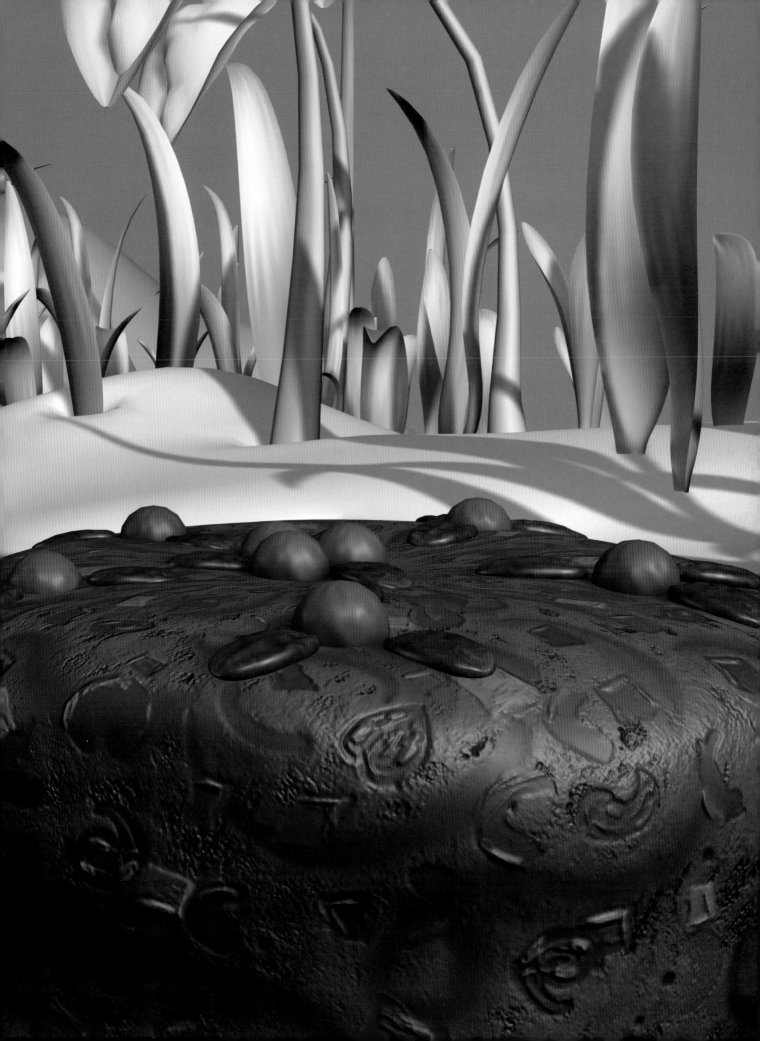

As the ants carried Grannypillar's Christmas fruitcake to the center of the garden, all the bugs gathered to watch and cheer.

Tomorrow would be Christmas Eve, and everyone would meet to sing songs and eat fruitcake.

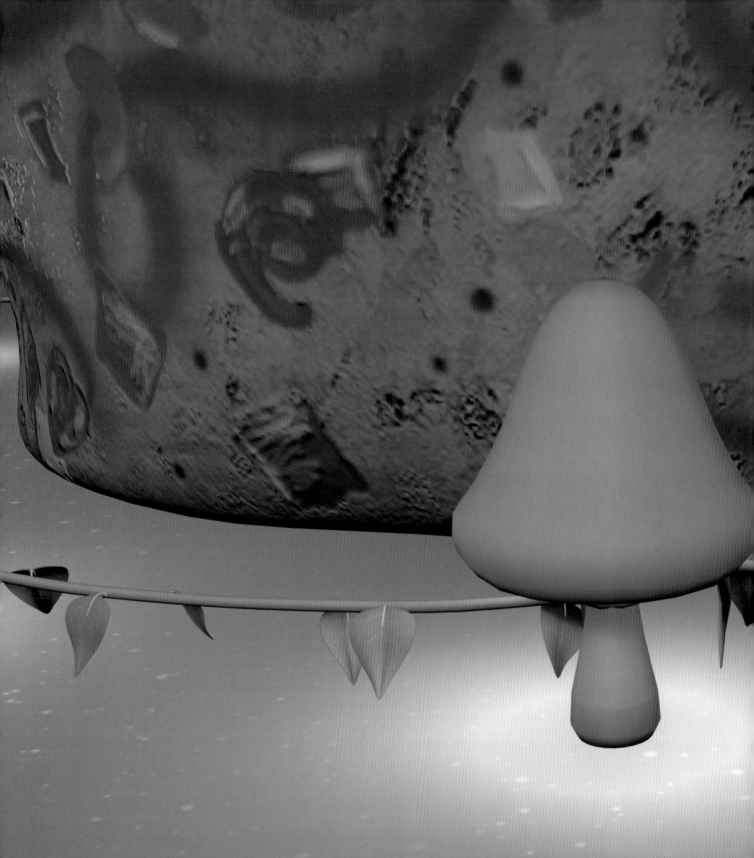

That night, AI and Art guarded the cake while everyone else slept. But—

WHOOPS! *K-Smack . . . K-Smack . . .*

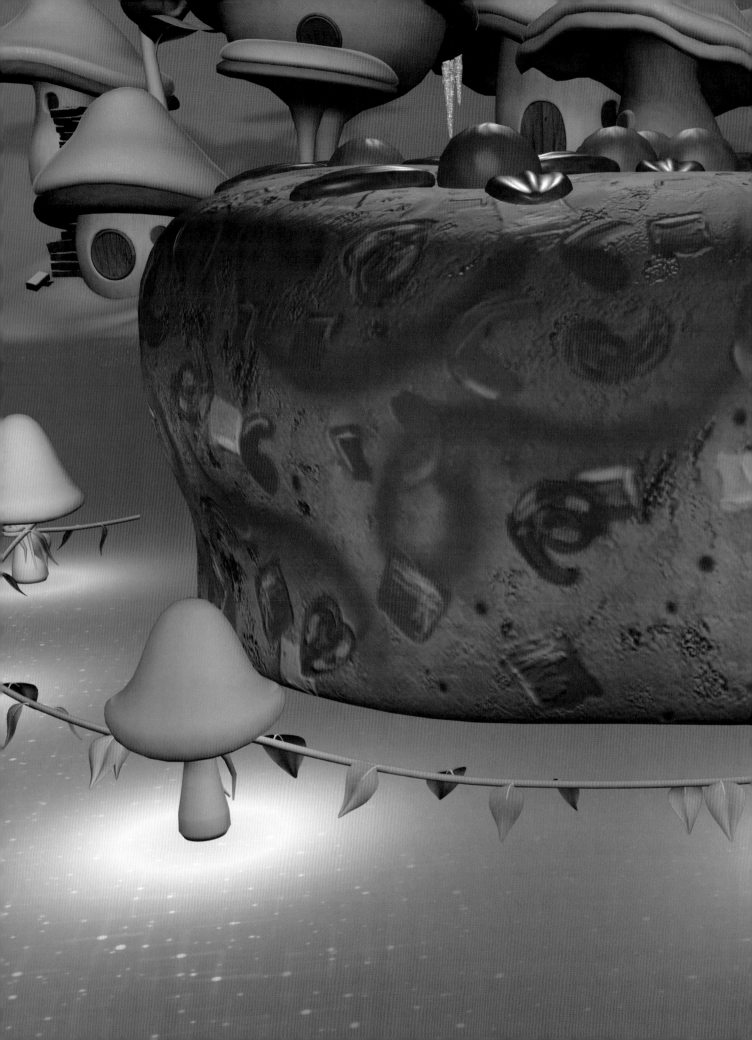

Kerplunk!

Al and Art accidentally
bumped into each other.

And while no one was
guarding the cake . . .

It Disappeared!

The garden friends were flabbergasted.
This had never happened before. Who could
have done such a mean and selfish thing?

"It must have been the cockroaches!" said Milt the Caterpillar. "They've taken everything else."

Everyone was very sad. Without the fruitcake, there could be no Christmas—or so they thought.

"We've got to get the fruitcake back!" they said.

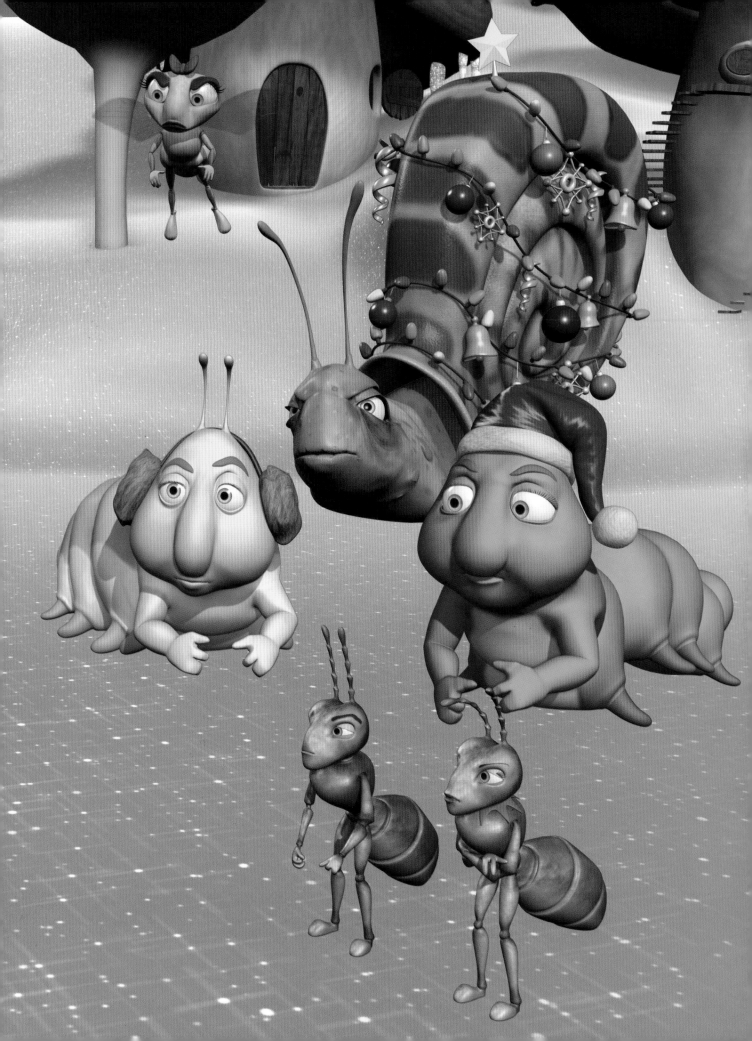

Cockroach
Mansion

Bedford Falls

Big Boy Bluff

RiverPool

The garden friends chose Hermie
and Wormie to go to Cockroach
Mansion. They would ask Iggy and
Ziggy to give the fruitcake back.

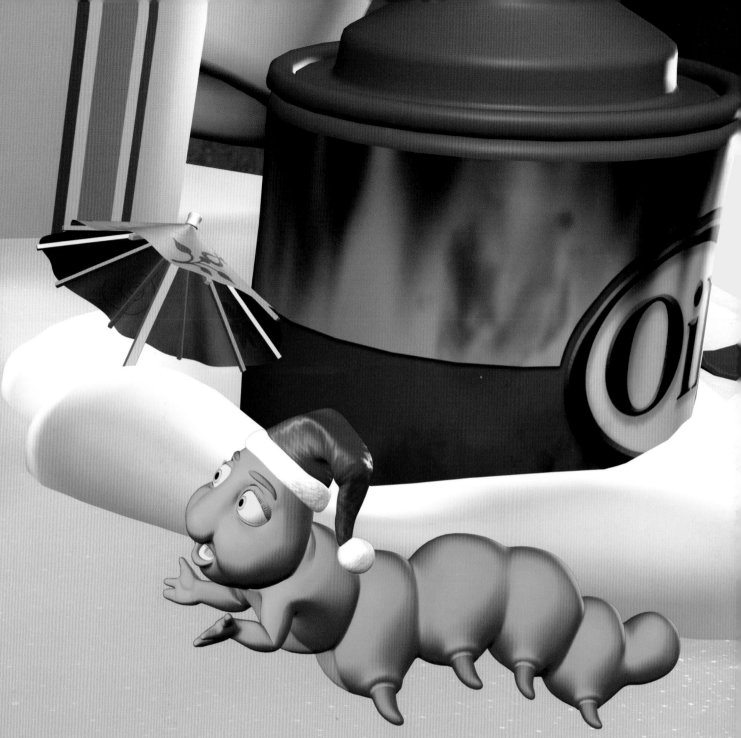

"Excuse me," Hermie said. "Our fruitcake is missing. Do you maybe . . . uh . . . have it?"

"Bah, humbugger. We don't have your fruitcake!" Ziggy lied.

"Go away," Iggy said. The cockroaches went inside, and **K-Blam** slammed the door shut.

Hermie and Wormie went back down the hill.

"What are we going to do?" Hermie asked.

Hailey and Bailey flew forward. "Maybe we should ask God."

"That's a great idea!" Hermie said. "God, how can we get the fruitcake back?"

God answered, "The fruitcake is nice, but it is not what Christmas is about. Christmas is about My gift to you—Jesus."

All the garden friends were sorry that they had made a fruitcake more important than God's gift.

Then Grannypillar found a small, old fruitcake
she'd forgotten about. There was only enough
for everyone to have one tiny piece.

The twins wanted to invite Iggy and Ziggy, but
the others only laughed. This made the twins
sad. But they had an idea. . . .

Hailey and Bailey made their way to Cockroach Mansion.

Iggy opened the door.

"What do you want?" Ziggy growled.

"We brought you a Christmas gift," Bailey said.

Hailey and Bailey gave their pieces of fruitcake to the cockroaches. No one had ever given Iggy or Ziggy a gift before—no one, not ever.

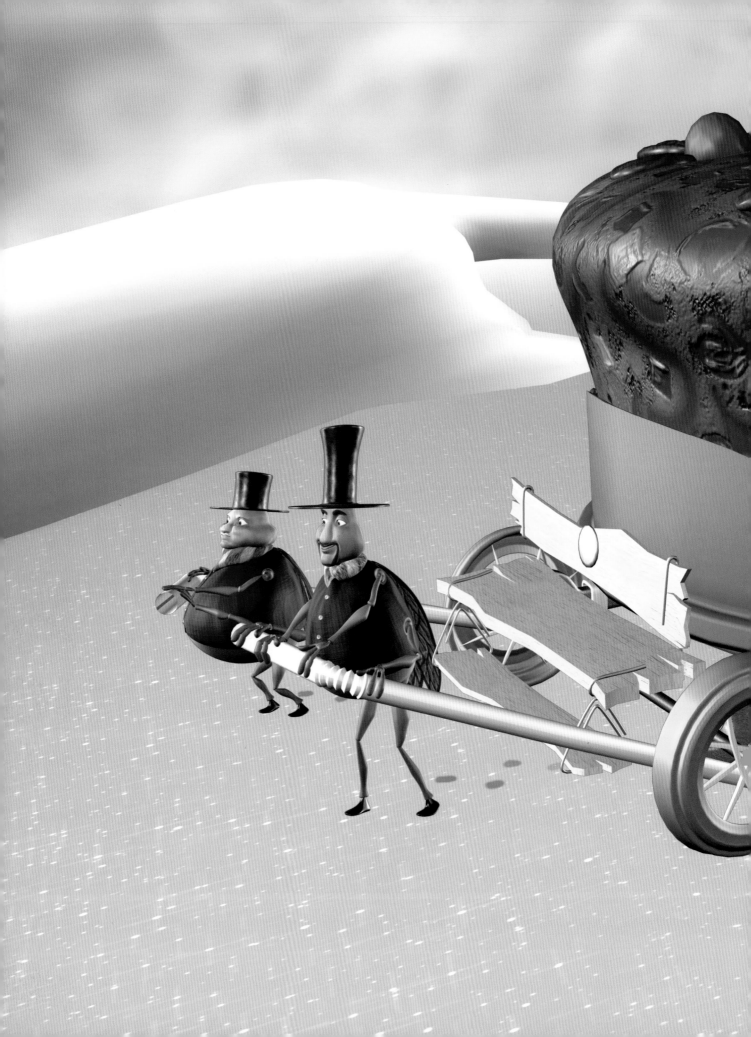

The twins' kindness made the cockroaches sorry for all the mean, selfish things they had done. They loaded up the cake, tossed in some extra nuts and fruit, and ran to the Christmas Eve celebration. They even let Freddie Flea have the day off.

Everyone was surprised when the cockroaches arrived with the fruitcake.

"We're sorry for taking the cake," Iggy said. "We didn't know Christmas is about giving, *not* getting, until Hailey and Bailey showed us."

"Will you forgive us?" Ziggy asked.

"YES!" the other bugs said. Then they did something the cockroaches never expected. . . .

They said they were sorry, too. "We were wrong not to invite you," Hermie said. "Will you join us to celebrate God's gift of Baby Jesus, and share our food?"

"Yes," said Iggy and Ziggy.

Lucy was proud of Hailey and Bailey. Their kindness to the cockroaches showed everyone how to share God's love with others.

And so, as the garden friends celebrated Christmas Eve, everyone understood that God's gift of Baby Jesus was the very best gift of all.